A novella by Cléo de Vigne

DM Publications

DM Publications
DM Design&Media SAS
67000 Strasbourg
Legal deposit (Bibliothèque nationale, Paris): October 2022

Translation: David Crowe
Print edition: ISBN 978-2-9583724-•-•
Electronic edition: ISBN 978-2-9583724-•-•
First printing: September 2022
Printed in Slovakia

To Bernard Weigel,

the best teacher I ever had.

The characters and situations in this story are purely fictitious. Any resemblance to actual persons, living or dead, is purely coincidental.

Prologue

It was a Wednesday morning shortly after ten o'clock when Norman Puttock walked briskly across the broad avenue that separated the run-down street where he lived from that on the opposite side of the park, which, according to the Greater London Statistics Office, was a considerably better place to live, do one's shopping and, naturally, enjoy one's ten o'clock constitutional attired in a tailor-made suit and a 60s-style brown homburg.

Puttock was a man of modest height – some would say very modest. He was built unevenly, a rotund body mounted on a pair of stick-like legs which served only to accentuate his stocky torso. Baldness had come early to him. Of his red hair there remained little; and what was left had already taken on an unpleasant yellowish tinge, a sign that the hair had aged faster than its owner.

Seeing him like that, with his upright walk, his proud aspect and his elegant apparel, the casual onlooker might have imagined great things of

Norman. That he must be a humanist of some sort, a philosopher or a writer, or a combination of the two. Or perhaps a scientist, equally at home in books of theory as in the laboratory, where he worked on great discoveries of world importance which would ensure that the name of Norman Puttock would find its place in the universal chronicles of collective knowledge.

Indeed, he believed fervently that he was all that, and more. On his engraved business cards one could read: *N.L. Puttock – writer, explorer, historian, photographer.* And there lay the source of his misery: with the passage of time the image he had of himself corresponded even less to the reality. Although only in his early forties, he seemed far older than his years. His eyes had a profoundly sad and defeated look, a certain ill-concealed resentment, sometimes with a plaintive touch, but always revealing an underlying bitterness.

The morning stroll was his opportunity to escape from the building where he had lived for the last fifteen years, a hideous place that he heartily detested. His flat was on the top floor of an old house in which several occupants had their separate rooms. He was proud that his status as a long-standing tenant had earned him a slightly larger room, with the added luxury of a minuscule kitchenette equipped with a refrigerator and microwave oven.

In this gloomy bedsit reigned a permanent, chaotic disorder. Amongst uncountable piles of books, old films, magazines and diverse bric-à-brac covered by dust could be discerned a table, almost invisible owing to the objects accumulated over many years and now lying on or against it. A single bed, its sheets creased and sliding to the floor, was half-hidden by dozens of bespoke shirts and jackets suspended from a metal rail above it. The scene was completed by a toothbrush which had somehow found a space for itself, a plant sitting on the floor, boxes of shoes, and a window left slightly open in a vain attempt to lessen the vile odour of stale smoke that had impregnated every fibre of the room. This was where Norman Puttock lived. He would don one of the suits which hung above the bed and walk out into the street – the epitome of the English gentleman.

He worked as a part-time administrator in a London-based organisation; it paid badly, and brought him no intellectual satisfaction. He encouraged his colleagues to believe he moved in high social circles, leading a life full of pleasurable moments and delightful outings to London's most chic establishments. In reality, he had neither the financial resources nor the necessary companions. The few occasions he had visited a grand restaurant had left him with costly memories that filled his dreams while at the same time creating a great sadness in him.

His literary ambitions had driven him long ago to start writing a book. (Indeed, this was his principal approach when he tried to impress the opposite sex.) He wanted so much to believe in himself as a writer that he lived this fantasy in an almost physical way – which made it all the easier for him to affirm without embarrassment that it was true. Over the years he had created for himself an imaginary persona that he did his best to live up to. He believed himself to be highly intelligent and a fount of knowledge, but the knowledge was superficial, for he had never studied; all his supposed erudition came from the books and the magazines of which he was an avid reader. So his understanding of the sciences was heavily influenced by his enthusiastic perusal of the *New Scientist*, in whose veracity he placed an unquestioning faith. He did, in fact, see himself as a man of science; and not a common one, rather as a respected researcher carrying out pioneering work. Pushed by megalomania he had a vision of himself as one of the elite, among whom he shone with an exceptional brilliance. Often, buoyed up by his self-centred folly, he engaged in violent arguments, finding unbearable the idea that anyone could hold a view different from his own.

His mental instability led him to drink; to drink a lot, in order to anaesthetise the deep-felt doubts in himself. He could be considered an alcoholic, being unable to function without the support of the bottle. This created great difficulties on those occasions when he had to face the world sober. Mornings were especially hard. He was incapable of speaking or acting normally, often preferring the unhealthy silence his abstinence produced. Then there was work, the curse of his life that he loathed with all his being. He detested his colleagues, their thoughts and their clothes. In his mind these people were scum. He himself was the only man worthy of respect. This dark truth depressed him horribly and made him nervous and aggressive.

Puttock's nature was curiously contradictory. Full of uncertainty, yet incredibly arrogant. So many things were wrong about him that he seemed like some vague project embarked on but never finished. The years would pass without his book advancing one iota. He was gnawed by solitude, but incapable of striking up friendships – still less a relationship with a woman. His life was at a standstill, caught somewhere between stultifying indolence and ambitious pretension. He had been undergoing psychiatric treatment for depression for several years. Depression, for him, was the cause of all his failings. Nothing was the fault of Norman Puttock; it was somebody else, it was the government, his boss, the weather or – above all – his depression. When he failed to keep a promise, it was because he was depressed. When he was embarrassed to tell the truth he fell easily into a lie. After all, it was not his fault, simply his depression. He did not even know what it was to be honest, he had lived a lie ever since he could remember, and had always used his depression as an excuse for the harm he did. Perhaps the only positive thing about the man was the very pretence that surrounded him, the deceptive charm inculcated by his perfectly observed mannerisms that so often bordered on the ridiculous. His sartorial style was the result of detailed studies, and he had worked to perfect his accent. And yet the more he took on for himself the role of irresistible dandy the worse his depression became. At times he looked at himself in the mirror and wept. He hated his body, and could not understand the injustice of it. Why him, why not someone else?

'Why me?' The question he asked himself several times a day. Why was he going bald, why didn't he earn enough, why had his wife left him, why was he born ugly? Why couldn't he live in a smart area, instead of having to share shower and toilets with illiterate idiots in the stinking house where he had his bedsit, his beautiful jackets hanging above his head while he slept and dreamt of being someone else? Why had he no friends, why were people so unkind to him (innocent lamb that he was), why did they resent him, look down on him – for the colour of his hair, for his name, for his diminutive stature, his round belly, his crooked teeth? Why had he never been accepted? Naturally, believing himself to be perfect, he assumed the rest of humanity was horrible.

Over the course of time he had developed his tastes and preferences by imitating others. Whatever people whom he considered to have taste and culture liked, he liked. He drank the cocktails enjoyed by the chic middle class. Despite his lack of cultivation and *savoir-faire* he adapted quickly, passing himself off as a connoisseur. The women he coveted had to be the women who were desired by all; what attracted him most was bling and popularity. His taste for the superficial determined all his choices in life, including in the matter of women. Being a repressed alpha male, the idea that other men would envy him gave him unparalleled satisfaction. Yet he never realised, or rarely, that he had nothing to offer in return. Not only was he poor, he was also stingy. What he needed – nay, what he had the right to – was a rich woman. The image he cherished of himself as a socialist humanitarian, despising materialism and capitalism in general, was a hollow one. Sometimes, walking past the shop-windows of Kensington High Street, he would catch sight of his reflection in the glass. Then he would stop, breathe a pitiful sigh, and laugh at himself. In truth he was obsessed by wealth and the recognition of wealth. Beneath his tweed suit and his hang-dog air lay an abject personality motivated by primitive desire and ignorant of any fellow-feeling. Lacking all decency and virtue, he gouged a path through life exploiting situations and people as he saw fit. In contrast to the idea that he had of himself, in reality his being was a dim little light kept alive by lies and hypocrisy. ☙

The rise of Norman Puttock

'SHIT!', HE EXCLAIMED. HIS GAZE was fixed on the fine leather sole of his beautiful shoe. He had to face it: the shoe was already ruined, planted as it was firmly in the middle of a dog turd. At least, he hoped the substance was of canine origin. His eyebrows came together in an expression that combined disgust with self-pity.

His mouth forming an irregular curve, he gave vent to a spiteful scream, like that of a pig having its throat slit. This unwanted misadventure had completely spoilt his peaceful stroll. For it was his habit to walk through London's streets, dressed to the nines, his movements supple and refined, his head held high – exceedingly high, as if to demonstrate the importance that providence had bestowed on him. He resembled a bird of paradise in the mating season. Watching his progress, one had the impression that he was dancing, bobbing up and down from time to time, waltzing to the rhythm of his own *amour propre.* Until that unfortunate accident that had jolted him out of his reverie to face a most disagreeable reality.

As he attempted, using a leaf picked up from the ground, to scrape off the faecal matter that seemed to have spread itself over his whole sole, he could not help but think of what a ridiculous spectacle he must portray at that moment. Overweight, and in poor physical shape as he was, the effort involved in bending over while standing on one leg caused him to perspire and gasp like a seal. Rivulets of sweat trickled down his creased forehead, and his back bent under the heavy weight of the constant anguish that had accompanied him throughout his life.

The air stank; and his life also stank. Except that, this Wednesday morning, N.L. Puttock's only point of interest was his shoe and the turd that clung to it. All his thoughts were circumscribed, like those of the most simple of minds, for which appearance signified being and for whom mediocrity was elevated to the level of the notion of absolute beauty.

'Mister! Please, mister! I'm so hungry!' came the plaintive voice, followed by a trembling arm that reached towards his horrified face. An ill-washed old woman, leaning on a plastic walking stick and with a red bandana on her head, was making gestures of despair, repeating over and over again, 'Please, mister, help me'.

'Filthy beggars,' was the thought that went through his mind.

He gritted his teeth. He was incapable of looking the woman in the eye, as if in fear of discovering himself in her wretchedness. The manifest disgust that filled his whole body terrified him. In his view, the city should be cleansed of all such parasites and the squalor they brought to the streets. Purely for aesthetic reasons, he said.

Immobile, not knowing what to do or say, mute and sadly insignificant, he looked around in palpable despair.

In that instant his eyes caught sight of a nearby pub, with tables set up before a wall painted in typical colours – mint green, blue and red – and hanging baskets from which flowed geraniums and purple and yellow pansies. Squinting through his glasses he was able to make out the name *The White Hart.*

The thought of a change of scene filled him with such boundless enthusiasm that he could not prevent himself from uttering, in the most disdainful way he knew, 'Go away and get a job, for heaven's sake!' And with that he turned his back and stalked away, his head high as if nothing untoward had happened.

Inside the pub the atmosphere was calm and hushed. Large solid oak tables stood around an oval bar. Floral wallpaper dotted with roses and peonies, a stray heron here, a pheasant there, adorned the walls and gave the room a country feel. At this time of the day there were few customers. Regulars would be coming later, around lunchtime, and would stay sipping their pints and reading their newspapers well into the afternoon.

Puttock slipped through the wide wooden entrance with exaggerated nonchalance, adopting a Bohemian disregard. As he made his way towards the bar, he alone was aware of the effort it cost him to seem so indifferent. He needed a drink to stop the perspiration running down his forehead. With clammy hands he raised the glass of ale to his lips.

Now life was rosy again! Once more he saw his future filled with great exploits. He felt his blood warming, his face regaining its habitual pinkness, the rhythm of his breathing stimulated by his ambition. Suddenly his eyes were drawn to a small poster pinned to a beam in the middle of the room. From a distance he tried to guess what it might be, his poor eyesight preventing him from reading anything but the word *urgent*, printed in bold and underlined twice. His curiosity growing, he went over to see more closely. *Narcissistic Idiots' Club seeks president*, he read.

Back at his table, he was overwhelmed by a feverish agitation. He was again perspiring, but now it was caused by the excitement he had felt in reading that simple sentence. His cheeks were burning, his eyes bulging and he was panting like a bull confronted by the matador's cape. Thunderstruck, he felt completely intoxicated. 'President,' he murmured.

From that instant on he just knew his life would take a new tack. He felt that the long years of misery were coming to an end. Soon his extraordinary capacities would have the recognition they deserved. 'President,' he muttered again and again into his beard, seeing nothing of what was happening around him. At that precise moment he was aware only of himself – the future president of the Narcissistic Idiots – and the thought created in him an almost mystical exultation.

But first he would have to win them over. The idea that he could gain a position of power made him giddy. Until then he had been completely unremarkable. Only a few days previously he had had another rejection letter from a publishing house. He was making no progress with his book, for which he was entirely lacking in inspiration. Needless to say, the storyline was uninteresting, taking as its central character none other than Puttock himself. His apathy for his own life made itself felt more and more frequently in the imaginary one and the influence on his writing was manifest. Blinded by bitterness, he had been losing his bearings. Now that he had something to live for, his strength was returning, reinforcing more than ever the belief that he was a genius.

THE DAY OF THE ELECTION dawned. Puttock had not slept a wink that night, and the morning had begun badly. He had planned to wear his best three-piece suit; but had been unable to button the waistcoat, his vast belly squeezed on one side by the waistband of his trousers and on the other by the braces that dug into his flabby flesh as if it were soft jelly. He stared angrily at his reflection in the mirror. Finally, having downed a double whisky, he donned the only suit that he could fit into and went down to the waiting taxi in the street below.

An hour later he found himself in an east London meeting-room rented for the occasion. From his place in the first row he stared curiously at the agitated throng. A high table and a microphone stood on a small platform at the front of the room. To the left and right of the seating area were set out drinks and cakes provided by members of the club. Colourful posters dotted around the room bore alluring slogans such as 'Proud to be a dickhead', 'God save the cretins' and 'Once an idiot, always an idiot'. A small cassette player from the 1990s playing bawdy songs was making its contribution to the ambience, which rose a notch each time one of the members raised his glass and cried 'Here's to stupidity!'

A tall man with white hair stepped on to the platform. He was wearing a red, two-piece tracksuit and carried a walking stick under his right arm. Beneath his tracksuit top he had a white vest, from which tufts of grey hair could be seen peeping out. On his chest dangled a pair of spectacles attached to a cord around his neck. Gradually the hubbub in the room died down to allow the man, who was clearly well known, to speak. He took a folded paper out of his pocket, then put on his glasses, which he rubbed fiercely against his nose, as if trying to find the best possible angle of view.

'Members, friends, welcome,' he intoned solemnly. 'We are here today to elect a new president. But before we do that, let us pay tribute to our late president, Mr Arthur Boulieu, an exceptional idiot. May he rest in peace.'

His voice trembled, signalling the gravity of his utterance. He took a deep and loud breath before continuing.

'He it was, and his acts, that were an inspiration to our club for years. He it was who frequently punctured his neighbour's tyres, who could drink seven pints of Guinness in four minutes and fifty-five seconds, who, the morning after the terrorist attacks in London sang *Hellbound Train*, at the top of his voice, in a carriage on the Bakerloo line.'

There was applause, together with whistles and ecstatic cries of joy.

'Yes, finding someone able to replace dear Boulieu will be difficult.' His voice trailed off into a sort of sigh culminating in an inevitable silence. After a short pause he resumed, this time infusing his speech with a false enthusiasm.

'Today, however, we are here to turn the next page of our life together. We have many applicants for the post of president of our club. I think we can all agree that the successor to dear Boulieu will have to be a man of outstanding idiocy. Only an absolute cretin, more egregious even than Boulieu, can maintain the status of our club at the highest level. And, as you all know, we are the best!'

This speech was greeted by roars of approval, and chants of 'Yes, yes, we are the best!' broke out on all sides.

With a look of surprise on his face, Norman

Puttock awaited with stupefaction the next phase in this strange process.

'What idiots,' he thought. Indeed, he felt a visceral disgust for the assembled crowd. But curiously, their idiot behaviour disturbed him less than their sartorial preferences. To his mind, a bad sense of style was the most conclusive proof of stupidity. Men in sandals, women in pink leggings and white tank tops, flip-flops in every colour of the rainbow. To Puttock, that was beyond the pale: flip-flops weren't just an error of judgement, they were the height of bad taste.

Next came the presentation of the candidates. Each was allotted ten minutes to set forth his or her ideas and distinguished opinions.

Puttock was feeling more and more nervous. He had always found exams stressful, and he hated the notion of competition. A mixture of thoughts ran riot in his head. How to impress this crowd of morons without revealing his contempt for them? His head was burning, and a bulging vein throbbed visibly on his bald pate. He found himself caught midway between euphoria and repulsion. As in a bad dream, he heard his name being called without being able to say where the sound came from.

This was his state of emotional turmoil as he made his way towards the podium. From behind the high table he looked out on the crowd. His view was blurred, shadowy shapes moved before his eyes, sounds became hazy and he felt on the verge of passing out.

'My dear idiots! Good morning,' he said, in a quavering voice. 'It gives me enormous pleasure to be here with you today. My name is Norman Puttock and I am, like you, a confirmed idiot. I believe that I have exactly the profile you are looking for, and I aim to prove it.'

The audience was silent, but he felt instinctively that he was on the right track. Gradually, his voice regained strength, and he scented, as it were, a light, intoxicating fragrance that gave him courage. His head a little higher now, he continued his speech.

'Take a good look at me. When I walk down the street, everyone turns to stare. Tramps seem to importune me more than they do anyone else; old ladies in Waitrose want to touch my hat; and mothers with children bestow their lubricious smiles on me. I am a most cultivated man: I know everything there is to know about cockroaches and hornets, about antimatter and about the bacteria that cause diarrhoea. My talents surpass by far those of a normal person: I am a writer, historian, scientist, photographer, theatre director, artist, musician, dancer. People tell me I have a unique sense of humour and – to tell the truth – I do have a tendency to crack up laughing when I see someone slip and fall. It's even funnier when it's an old, disabled person.'

Laughter rang throughout the hall.

'Even our prime minister – a remarkable person, whom I admire greatly – has been known to laugh at my jokes.'

There were more cheers.

'But it is time to speak of the initiatives I'd like to carry out, with your help, dear members. I wish to invest my own money in this club, as a registered business.'

As the words left his mouth he sniggered inwardly at the ludicrous lie. He was, in fact, a mean, tight-fisted man with a soul steeped in stinginess. His lack of generosity could be seen not only in his attitude to money, but also in affairs of the heart – an organ whose only purpose in his body was to deal out the heartbeats in order to prolong his ignoble existence. With mounting excitement, he continued.

'What this club needs is prestige, class and intelligence. I have great ideas for its future. As president I shall do all in my power to make us known throughout the country. I shall launch a publicity campaign to attract sponsors. I shall apply for grants from the mayor of London and request a bigger budget from the Chamber of Commerce. We shall issue our own publication – The Idiot's Manifesto – printed on deluxe silk-finish paper and on sale in bookshops.

'This club has tremendous promise, and I have grand ideas for it. In my view, we have a good chance of becoming an unstoppable force in the life of this country. And this is why, my dear imbeciles, this is why I insist that you must elect me as your president. I see it as my duty to guide you and accompany you on our future journey together.

'And before I finish, I should like to assure you that I would be perfectly capable of singing *Hell-bound Train* in the Tube; and not only that, but I would add a little dance to complete the scene!'

At this, the crowd could no longer control itself, as the intoxicating atmosphere got the better of even the most sober of the members.

'I call on you, then, with all my power: idiots of the world, unite!'

The room vibrated with frenetic applause and admiring shouts. It was a triumph. Nothing existed before his speech, nor after, he was master of time and space, the crowd could see only him. His head was spinning.

Out in the street he needed a few minutes to gather himself together. His mind was still drowning, faced with the sweet chimera of success. He walked like an automaton, his destination unknown. His being overflowed with *amour propre*, he felt so powerful and so physically spellbinding that he yearned to cover himself with his own kisses.

But once back in his smoky den his anger returned in force. The gloomy context in which he found himself was far from that which he felt he deserved. The background odour of burnt grease and tobacco was complemented by a pervasive smell of curry. Perched on his tiny sofa, he greedily gobbled down his Indian take-away. He chewed vigorously, and interspersed his bouts of belching with copious gulps of wine. He had removed the constricting trousers, and his badly buttoned shirt barely covered the deformed belly which hung down over his grubby Y-fronts like a a melting ball of suet. He could not get out of his head the memories of that extraordinary day, the raised voices and the glowing faces.

In all his life he had never felt so desirable. In the end, he thought, I am not so ugly and insignificant.

He rose slowly to his feet, removed his clothes, and stepped towards a tall mirror hidden in a dark recess. For several long minutes he stared intently at his reflection. Seeing himself naked triggered in him a sort of carnal reflex. He caressed his flabby body, giving forth short, sharp cries. His hands trembled; his breathing accelerated. With bestial groans he kneaded his swollen penis mercilessly, until at last he achieved the long-awaited satisfaction.

Exhausted by this unforeseen effort he lay on the bed looking at the ceiling.

'President ... I am the president,' he murmured, savouring each syllable.

FOUR WEEKS HAD PASSED SINCE the day of the election. Puttock had resigned from his job with a flamboyant gesture, presenting a huge bouquet of flowers to his superior, whom he heartily detested. He had shaken hands all round with his male colleagues and hugged the women. He had even made a short speech saying he was heartbroken to leave but that was how life had worked out: his departure was inevitable because a greater duty awaited him.

And he firmly believed it. If only he were not so lazy. Despite everything, his life was changing. Hitherto a completely insignificant creature, he was becoming a personality known, at least, in certain Fitzrovia restaurants and a few Savile Row tailors. He had settled into a routine. On Mondays he would sleep late before breakfasting on an espresso and a croissant – to convey the insouciant air of a Frenchman, he told himself. Afterwards he would head for the chic districts of

London. Crossing Regent's Park he would emerge in Marylebone, pausing occasionally at pavement cafés before continuing towards Buckingham Palace. Then he would stroll casually around Covent Garden. The other days of the week were spent in a similar fashion, apart from Wednesdays, which were devoted to his duties at the club of which he now found himself the respected president. Here he delivered his weekly report to the distinguished members. He was so appreciated by the latter that they showered him with gifts and privileges. From the men he had bottle-openers, Swiss knives and free tickets to football matches. The women brought him apple pie and homemade biscuits. Unfortunately he hated sport and detested sweet things; and so all these unwanted gifts he presented to the centre for the homeless a couple of streets away from his new workplace. Thus he garnered a reputation as a good and charitable person, moved by the unenviable plight of the hundreds of occupants of the centre. When he dropped by with his bags full of sweetmeats and other trivial goodies he was welcomed with open arms and beaming faces. He was viewed as a kind of dandy-ish source of munificence who, despite his clearly overpriced suit and his snobbish, capricious behaviour, put them in mind of their own miserable condition.

'My dear Gladys, here you are!' He could not help patronising the beneficiaries of his largesse; and the more he despised the person in question, the more flagrant was his superficial kindness. 'I've brought you a lovely cheesecake, some oranges, kiwi fruit and three muffins. Make sure you give them to those who have behaved themselves, ha, ha!' His loutish tone rang out through the room. Gladys, who ran the centre, had heard remarkable stories about her benefactor. Word had got out, and all sorts of rumours were circulating. It was said that Puttock was a descendant of a noble line who wanted to keep his origins a secret. He had supposedly studied in the best universities in the country, and held a multitude of degrees in an extraordinary range of subjects. It was even rumoured that he was capable of demonstrating the flaws in the theory of relativity.

'Thank you, Mr Puttock. We are all so grateful. You are our favourite benefactor, you know. We adore you, and we'll always be delighted to welcome you.' She leant forward, as if bowing before some deity whose gaze she was afraid to meet.

'Oh! I nearly forgot the most important thing.'

From his messenger bag he pulled out a plastic sachet, shaking it so that its contents rattled. 'Here are some badges from the club that I'm president of. You can share them, give them away. Don't worry, gorgeous Gladys, there's plenty more if you need them. Just let me know. Here, put one on.' And without waiting for a reply, with a flourish he pinned one of the badges to the lapel of her jacket. On it could be read: 'Complete moron'.

Since his first visit to the neighbourhood he had taken to frequenting a hostelry with the picturesque name of Ye Olde Suckling Pig. The staff and the other regulars knew him as 'the president' or 'the boss'. Here it was that he spent whole days sometimes, drinking and holding forth before the bewildered eyes of the clientele.

That day it was raining heavily. It had rained all night, and the day promised to be grey and chilly. Puttock, seated at a table for four looking out on to the street, was pretending to read. But in reality he was observing the passers-by hurrying to escape the inclement weather.

A portly man, walking with a crutch, made his way to the table where Puttock, his legs crossed, was already consuming his aperitif. The man, supported on one side by his crutch, held in his other hand a pint of bitter which slopped around in time with his irregular movement. Groaning from the effort he took a seat opposite Puttock.

The man was Caspar Finley, an ex-MP with a passion for horse-racing and detective stories. He and Puttock had become acquainted in this very pub one well-lubricated evening, when Puttock had given vent to one of his endless rants about fleas, micro-organisms and the global conspiracy of the secret societies of the rich.

'My dear Finley, I was just thinking of you.' His tone was even more affected than usual. 'I have something important to discuss with you. I hope you don't mind, but I've also asked the Glimowitz brothers to join us.'

As if on cue, two men entered the bar. One was small and hunched, his dry skin patterned with prominent veins. He had a long salt-and-pepper beard together with a baseball cap worn backwards. The other was tall and athletic, his beard neatly trimmed and his hair thinning to reveal an incipient bald patch.

'And here they are! This way, my friends!' His extravagant hand-gestures were in perfect contrast to the detachment displayed by the new arrivals.

'I asked you all here because I have something

to propose to you.' He paused reflectively before continuing.

'As you know, I am president of a club with enormous potential.' His companions could not prevent the slightly mocking smiles that appeared momentarily on their otherwise serious faces.

'I shan't beat about the bush. Here's what I have in mind.'

Animated by an unaccustomed energy, Puttock stood, as if to indicate his superiority over the trio, who remained unmoved and unmoving in their seats.

'I'm going to turn my club into a national force. I'm going into politics.'

The astounded Finley almost choked on the mouthful of beer he had just taken. The Glimowitz brothers stared vacantly at him, not even blinking. It was not the reaction Puttock had expected to his solemn declaration.

'My friends, I see you are surprised. And you are no doubt asking, "What does this have to do with us?" Well, I'd like to offer jobs to all of you. Finley, how would you like to be vice-president? And you two gentlemen, my right hand and my left hand?' His finger indicated first one of the brothers, then the other, pointing directly at their astonished faces.

As excited as a nervous kitten, he continued. 'This country needs me ... er, needs us. Look at this badge. I could sell it for five pounds, but it's worth only twenty-five pence. You see what I'm getting at?'

They stared at him incredulously.

He moved towards a small platform used as a stage when the bar organised stand-up shows, which it was wont to do every Friday during happy hour. This allowed the habitual drinkers to serve as an audience for the would-be comedians who were happy to be able to perform before anyone, even in a dive such as this.

'Oy, Percy, switch on the mike, and be quick about it!' Percy was the barman, waiter, receptionist and cleaner. With remarkable speed he activated the microphone, even adding a 'Right away, boss!'

Standing on this miniature podium, Puttock stretched his body as if to compensate for his rotundity. There was something aggressive in his pose. Like a peacock losing its feathers he attempted to make himself desirable for the masses of invisible spectators whom he imagined were watching him with envy and admiration. In fact his audience consisted only of Finley, the two brothers, and Percy the barman.

'One, two. One, two. Can you hear me?' He tugged his beige waistcoat towards his waistband, touched the knot of his tie and ran a hand over his misshapen skull.

'I had a mishap this morning. Broke my key in the lock. I had to make two trips to the locksmith. What a despicable and incompetent chatterbox! And he had the bloody nerve to charge me sixty-five quid, the wretch!

'But that's not what I wanted to talk to you about. Erm... oh, yes. It was pouring down, and I had to take a taxi to avoid spoiling my new shoes. Beautiful, aren't they? Made to measure. You can see it'd have been a disaster if they'd got wet. And the taxi driver – what a moron! Drove like a lunatic! I thought I was going to die in that crappy cab. I swear, he didn't even stop at the Abbey Road zebra crossing. You should have seen all those idiots busy taking selfies run like mad!'

Like that of a schoolboy, his cackling laughter echoed through the bar.

'Percy? Is the mike working? You can hear me, can't you?'

The barman nodded. But Puttock had run out of words. He needed a strong drink, maybe two or three. Sweating, he rubbed his moist palms together.

'Did I tell you I'm active in the homeless shelter? You really should see them when I turn up. Those ungrateful faces. You know, some of them have spots as if they were diseased. It's disgusting! But by now they must all be wearing our badge. Bound to improve their appearance!' He gave a full-throated laugh intermingled with small snorts. With a dismissive gesture he tossed the microphone to the ground and headed for the bar, where his dirty martini was already being prepared by the terrified barman.

Back at the table, he addressed his newly formed team.

'To my mind, we hold all the cards. The club's on my side, I've got all the down-and-outs of London. I'll go to all the shelters personally. They won't be able to resist my oranges and mince pies. You know you can get end-of-shelf-life stuff from supermarkets? I'll bring them eggs that aren't even rotten. Do you hear what I'm saying?

'And that's not all. I'll tour the country. I'll go meet people in every city. I already have invitations from the Blackpool Failed Anglers, the Milton Keynes Roundabout Appreciation Society and the Idle Working Men's Club in Bradford. We'll hold events that no one has done before. I'm going to cut the ribbon to open the first retirement home for dogs. Yes, I know that dogs can't vote. But their owners can! Imagine one of those furry balls with our badge on his doggy coat! Immoral, yes; but that's our aim. Isn't that right, Finley?

Finley, placidly enjoying his beer, feigned an interest.

'Yes, boss, that's our aim.'

The Glimowitz brothers remained silent. Unlike Finley, they seemed not to feel the need to show involvement.

Downing his cocktail in one, Puttock picked up his coat.

'I have to go now,' he announced solemnly. 'I have an amorous rendezvous with a divine creature.'

He donned his hat and ran his long fingers through his beard. Taking his pipe from his pouch he placed it in his mouth as if he were smoking it.

Then, apparently satisfied by this exaggerated pose, he left the bar, his vanity stimulated by an illusion of power hitherto unknown, and brought about by an absolute and all-conquering impression of being the centre of the universe.

AT ONE O'CLOCK PRECISELY HE pushed open the door of the restaurant where he was due to meet one of his numerous recent conquests. Since his rise to notoriety he had been enjoying some success with women, aided by a powerful self-confidence – even though he still trembled from head to foot if he so much as embarked on a conversation without a stiff drink inside him. Seeing that his date was not yet there, he took advantage of the fact to order a double scotch which he downed in one.

In fact, there was really only one woman who interested him: an aspiring music-hall dancer, whom he considered the height of perfection, far more than an ugly man like himself deserved. For years she had been the object of his fantasies, even during his marriage to the woman who was later to break his heart. That, at any rate, was the story he told; in reality his ex had simply gone off with another man and had broken nothing at all of him – except perhaps a part of his bloated ego. Motivated by a mixture of ill-will and avarice, he rejected her repeated requests for a no-fault divorce. One night at the Suckling Pig, drunk as a lord, he gave an embarrassing account of the logic behind his refusal. Standing on a chair with his tie askew and his flies half-undone, grunting like a pig, he held forth to all who would listen.

'I paid for the marriage, so she can damn well pay for the divorce.' (Needless to say, there was no truth in the assertion: he had not paid a penny before, during or after the marriage.)

'Her dad owns some of the oldest pubs in town and she's the only heir, the bitch! Just think, Finley – listen, now – if the old guy kicks the bucket she gets the lot. She'll be a millionaire! I can only hope that he snuffs it and she gets run down by a bus, or maybe a Morris 1000, who cares?'

That evening he had soiled his trousers in front of them all. They had carried him out to a taxi, which had deposited him in the street outside his apartment, and there he had spent the night, waking the next day with no memory of what had happened.

Now, however, his companion for this evening was at the door. He observed her in the distance and thought she was not as good-looking as the last time. He must have been drunk then; otherwise, why would he have invited her? Looking at her now he had absolutely no desire to sleep with her.

But a couple of drinks broke the ice, and soon they were talking of travel and insects. That is, she attempted to describe her last trip to the Caribbean while he monopolised the conversation, rambling on about the life and habits of bumblebees. After an hour's ordeal he took out his pocket watch and informed his unfortunate date that he had to leave urgently. In view of the delicate situation he felt obliged to pay, something which irritated him immensely. How unfair, he thought, having to pick up the bill for a woman he had no desire for. Why, even when he *was* interested he would always try to avoid paying.

A little later he was sitting on a bench in Fitzroy Square, filling his pipe between discreet sips of brandy from a flask taken from an inside pocket. In recent weeks on this same bench he had exchanged embraces with a number of women. It was his favourite haunt to take his prey, after the obligatory visit to the pub followed by a short evening walk: always the same three streets, in the same order, before ending up at the bench where he would declare his overwhelming love for the day's victim. He would give the first kiss, then make a passionate avowal of longing intended to convey his enormous sexual desire. And it had to be said that his scheme worked well: one out of two times he ended up in the bed of some floozy won over by his exotic and unclassifiable charm.

But despite this success he was not happy. On the one hand he could not rid his mind of the memory of Claire, the young dancer who was the only object of his lust. On the other, he was so self-conscious about his body that every sexual encounter was torture for him. He usually couldn't get an erection, let alone ejaculate. And even when he did, he was rapidly exhausted because of his poor physical condition. He knew how pitiful he was as a lover but, as with everything in life, he preferred to delude himself and believe the opposite. Except that in this situation it was extremely difficult for him to convince himself of what he wanted to be sexually.

He was addicted to masturbation and an avid consumer of pornography. For this reason he was unable to climax other than during his solitary activities. Most of the women he went to bed with felt sorry for him, and therefore tended to shower him with flattery. This avoided their having to explain why they had taken no pleasure in the bizarre experience and had faked their orgasms.

Some while ago he had taken up with a widow, aged but rich, and now spent much of his time with her. She had fallen under his innocent, angelic spell and had shown him great generosity. He lavished her with compliments and quoted mawkish nineteenth-century poetry. In the evening he would not go to bed without wishing her 'Good night, my dearest'; and in the morning he read Keats to her. From the very beginning he had imitated her way of speaking, her taste in food, even the way she exclaimed. A new world was opening to him. What's more, he was not required to sleep with her – or so he thought – and this reassured him greatly, terrified as he was by his lack of sexual prowess.

In the widow's company he would frequent the best restaurants, places of whose very existence he had been ignorant, and would find himself transported into a world beyond imagination, his senses pampered by luxurious pleasure. For the first time in his life he tasted caviar, Scottish smoked scallops and genuine Alba truffles. He attained the absolute peak of gastronomic decadence one evening when he drank absinth, with fountain and all the paraphernalia. That, to him, was the mark of success: to be able to move in the same circles as the London bourgeoisie and eat and drink well. To be personally idolised was merely a means of infiltrating that realm of luxury to which he had always aspired. In this world there was nothing better than a good meal in a fashionable restaurant – not forgetting the wine, which had to be vintage and beyond the reach of the common man. In conversation he passed himself off as a Marxist, a humanist deeply touched by social inequality and the injustices borne by the working class. The same working class, of course, which made him want to vomit and was a continual reminder of his own origins.

He was always the guest of someone, which caused him no embarrassment. Lacking all sense of dignity, he openly took advantage of his rich friends, convinced that this was his legitimate and absolute right. But even he was aware that this could not continue for ever and that very soon he would be obliged to return the favour. Like a leech he hung on, and tried to make the most of it. He would always choose the most expensive dish on the menu and order vintage champagne. He remained confident that this lady who was so generous to him would provide him with a small flat in central London; or at least bestow on him some of her considerable estate, which included a cottage in Surrey and a country house in Berkshire. Nevertheless, she was beginning to call him too often and to impose herself on him. Perhaps – and this is what he was most afraid of – she even hoped for physical relations with him. Suddenly he decided, with great regret, that he would have to get rid of her. But after feigning depression, suicidal tendencies and mysterious illnesses, he had to abandon his plan. Her heart and her compassion would not let her leave him.

'Josephine, my dear, you are my sun, my stars, my moon! How I shall miss you tonight!' he told her, holding her two hands which he covered in kisses. 'I would so much have liked to invite you home with me! If it were not for these dreadful renovations! But soon, I promise, very soon I shall show you my newly beautiful home. I'll spoil you with surprises! You'll see, my darling Josephine. I dream of taking you travelling, I live to make you happy, to see you smile; it's all I live for, my treasure. Have patience, my angel. It's my depression, it saps my energy, I'm weak, almost at death's door, and yet all I want is to be with you, to take you to

Venice on the Orient Express, to celebrate life ... with you, the most precious, the most magnificent creature in the universe.'

Until the day, in the near future, when the elderly lady heard no more from him. Like a rat he crept back to the familiar squalor of his den where he felt so much at home. And there he was destined to end his days – only he did not yet know it.

THUS WAS THE PATTERN OF his life, which was like a game to him. He would first woo his victim, then take financial advantage of her before finally faking a depression as a pretext to discard her. The ladies could not believe it, all wanting to help him, and not realising that this was the final act and that their part in this farce was coming to an end. Always the same words, the same tedious poetry readings, the same false compliments, and the same lamentable attempts at sex.

His new post as president and his political ambitions gave him the strength to overcome his genital demons, that nameless horror that had been dormant within him since his teenage years. His worst nightmare was to find himself naked in public. Sometimes he would awake drenched in sweat, screaming like a little girl, hoarse and trembling with terror.

In matters of sex his predilections were anything but those of a normal heterosexual man, a fact he knew all too well. He found women attractive, but was incapable of doing what an ordinary man would do. He wanted to be penetrated, dominated, humiliated if possible. But since he was at the same time extremely prudish, when he alluded to such practices in front of his mistresses he was often misunderstood.

He found some solace in pornography, but he would have liked to experience such things in real life. And so, one day, not far from his sordid abode, he ventured into a hostess club, despite the misgivings he held concerning this type of service.

Inside, it was unprepossessing and cold. A few women could be seen, sitting at the bar or on a shabby sofa by the wall, their legs crossed inexpertly and their gaze listless. He went up to what seemed to be a bar and ordered a whisky. A peroxide-blonde woman in her late forties, wearing a mini-skirt in imitation leather and a bra, gestured to him with her almost empty glass.

'Here's to you, darling!' Her bright red lips opened in a gappy smile. 'What's your fancy, then? Come on, love, you can tell me.'

Torn between embarrassment and curiosity, he did not know how to answer. He was thinking. A lot of questions were running through his mind and he felt as if he were playing the lead role in a sixties film noir.

'What will twenty-five quid get me?' he mumbled in a low voice. The blonde cackled, her laughter causing a general unease in the bleak surroundings.

'Twenty-five? That'll buy you a blow-job, kid. And a feel of me boobs. They're brand-new!' She laughed heartily, her breasts wobbling in time with her exertions.

'I need you to sit on my face. And for twenty more I want you to penetrate me and lick my ... er, you know what I mean.'

Before replying she looked around, as if to check that the place was dead and she wasn't going to miss a big catch.

'OK, you're sort of cute, and I feel sorry for you with your ratty teeth. Look at me, I ain't no better, put all I could afford into me new tits. One or the other it was, like in life: it's bacon or cheese, you know?' He nodded, but frowned as he considered her words.

She led him into a small room, gloomy and oppressive. It was perhaps just as well that he could not see much in the dark. It smelt of sperm and vomit and the essence of human suffering. In absolute silence he lay down on the couch placed in the middle of this strange place of physical ecstasy.

'Really press down. I want to feel suffocated, you understand? And at the same time put all your fingers in my rectum. And you have to cry out. I want to hear you scream with pleasure. Tell me I'm the best, the most handsome, wittiest, seductive, a sex-beast, a holy monster, a cosmic icon, absolutely heavenly and unique. Will you do all that while you do the other business, you know what I mean?'

'Got it, ducky! You're the best.'

And she stared at him like someone looking at a three-legged dog and wondering what had happened to the poor beast to get him into such a state.

His political party took off like a rocket. Nobody really knew how, but he had succeeded in reaching out to the masses. It was simply a fact: people liked him and wanted more of him. He was in demand at events, on TV programmes and at funfairs. He was the special guest every time a special guest was announced. His face could be seen on many a poster advertising products and brands of all kinds. He appeared on buses, in shop windows and even on one of the gigantic screens at Piccadilly Circus. The old ladies in Waitrose were no longer content to touch his hat; they wanted to take him in their arms and tell him how much he was like their late husbands. After the old ladies, it was the turn of the teenagers, who would stop him in the street to take a picture with him and ask for his autograph.

Assured of his success, he decided it was time to dump his string of useless mistresses and to set out to conquer Claire, the dancer. The promises he had made to the others, the carefully constructed lies, were no longer important. With his latest flame he had once again played the depressive card. Shortly before he was due to see her again he had claimed to be dying. Like a lost soul, he screamed about his misfortune on the telephone, ranting and raging about how terribly bad he felt. He even dared to blame his victim for being incapable of understanding him and of putting herself in his place.

'If you really loved me you'd give me a chance to recover my sanity so we could enjoy ourselves together. But for that I need time. I'd do that for you, because I adore you more than anything, and our love is the only thing that counts for me.'

Weeping, with a ridiculously high-pitched childish voice, he went on.

'You're the only important person in my life. I'm passionate about you; I always will be. But this depression is consuming me, eating me up, I have to keep my distance from you. I'm taking some very strong medicine and I've been feeling so tired recently. Don't take it wrong, my love. I'm exhausted, completely shattered. But I'm counting the days till I can be in your arms again. You're my only love, my precious stone that shines even in the deepest darkness.'

Yet scarcely a week later he was heading for Rules restaurant in London, his new conquest, the dancer, on his arm, proudly crossing the threshold like a distinguished regular of the sort who had been frequenting the establishment for over a century. His heart throbbed with excitement. For only a short time ago he had never heard of this elegant venue, and to go there in the company of the woman he had desired for so long gave him a divine pleasure. The fact that he had lied and stolen the idea from another never crossed his mind. He was a stranger to remorse, being concerned solely with his own satisfaction.

Such was Norman Puttock. An absolute fraud, a human cesspit filled with waste that he recycled and reused in whatever way suited him. He had transcended normal wickedness and become a many-headed hydra of deceit. Always the same poetry by Keats, the same verses, jokes, laughter, more poetry, fictitious stories of his past ... and tons and tons of lies.

It suited him perfectly to escort such a young woman, since she lacked the experience to assess him accurately. In addition, since he did have feelings for her, he made a great effort to conceal his true face, hiding behind a subtle brilliance the futile hypocrisy of his grotesque being.

At this point in his life he had the impression that he was a complete success – or almost. He enjoyed fame, recognition, and a stunning woman. All that he lacked was wealth. Despite all his machinations – embezzlement, abuse of party funds – he needed more. Once having tasted blood he was unable to live without it. The more he stole, the more he felt he was missing out on what he believed he naturally and fundamentally deserved. He was developing tastes more and more luxurious and his rapacious instincts were growing to the point where he could no longer control them. When he dined on steak he would order two; his dessert had to be adorned with edible gold leaf; and the least expensive champagne on the menu was simply not good enough. Waiters were required to bow down before him, otherwise he refused to enter the establishment. His employees addressed him as *my lord* or *your highness*. And the grey parrot he had bought had been trained to squawk 'the best in the world' every time he walked into the room.

He walked over corpses while maintaining his holier-than-thou air, convinced of his innocence and his miserable background, which for the most part was a figment of his imagination.

He tolerated only the rich. Anyone else was worthless scum. He was incapable of loving anyone, with the sole exception, perhaps, of his young mistress. But even this love had an expiry date, for fidelity was an unknown concept to him and he had a tendency to get bored very quickly.

One aim in life he followed very strictly: humiliate at least three people a day. If he succeeded, this would make his day. For instance, he would tell Finley he was ugly, kick a beggar's collecting jar or give rotten clementines to the homeless centre on purpose. He liked to make fun of taxi drivers' foreign accents, and never tipped but insisted on the last penny in change. He would then get out of the car feeling even more powerful than before. After that, his misdeeds would continue and his day would only get brighter. Sometimes, just for his own pleasure, he would discreetly take out his keys and scratch the luxury cars parked on the street.

He delighted in his hatred of humanity and rejoiced in the cult of his personality.

Little did he know that, in the midst of his selfishness and disdain for others, disaster awaited him. ☙

The fall of Norman Puttock

DAYS, WEEKS, MONTHS PASSED. NORMAN Puttock luxuriated in the pleasurable carefree atmosphere that he believed to be his new reality which could only get better. Especially his finances. The stipend he received from the club was modest. As leader of his political party he was paid fees and on occasion substantial sums for appearing in commercials, but his income did not go far towards covering his outgoings.

His greed and lack of self-respect made him willing to accept any offer going. The only criterion was the colour of the money. In his view bad publicity did not exist; the only things he valued were the fee and his celebrity.

'After all, I am the president of the Narcissistic Idiots, what worse could happen to me?' Such was the mantra by which he calmed himself.

For this reason he had lent his image to numerous advertising campaigns promoting diverse products. Anything, whether it was hearing aids or a shampoo to prevent hair loss was grist to his mill as long as the money was good.

At the same time his illicit deeds became more frequent, as did the number of bribes he accepted. He would conclude the stupidest deals and make the most unrealistic promises. In this way his interactions with the London underworld were strengthened, rapidly becoming his main source of revenue.

He started a business smuggling morel mushrooms, in the hope of making his fortune. The transport from Normandy, the sweeteners paid to customs officers, the distribution on the market – all was his responsibility, and he delighted in it. He produced fake import papers and sold the precious fungus at exorbitant prices. His morels gained such a reputation in Greater London that he acquired the sobriquet 'The Mushroom Magnate'.

In his private life his relationship with the dancing girl was fragile. Each of them wanted something different: he longed to be loved, whereas she was interested only in money and fame. The truth was that to her he was physically repulsive. His body odour and his feeble performances between the sheets did not help. She found him unbearable in bed. Sitting on his face, she could scarcely bear to look at him – his body bloated with drink and gluttony, his belly distended and firm as if he were about to give birth.

Occasionally, despite his inability to be a man in bed, he attempted penetration in the missionary position. This activity he found so exhausting that he felt close to fainting. His heart beat double-time, his breathing was heavy and noisy, and the whole act lasted less than a minute and would never end in ejaculation.

After one such disaster he invited her out to a chic restaurant in the vain hope of diverting her from his less than magnificent performance. Addled by drink, he attempted to explain. 'The problem is these anti-depressants. Dear heart, you're the best thing that ever happened to me!' She sipped her gin and tonic in silence and regarded him with an expression of pain and contempt.

The pair were in fact fundamentally similar. They shared common ideals centred around an enormous navel-gazing bubble, as pretentious as it was meaningless.

Both in their own way were cold and manipulative, with the rare ability to have absolutely no feelings for anyone else.

Self-centred, megalomaniac to the core, they nevertheless presented to the masses an image of elegant inaccessibility. In the end the glitzy exterior outweighed the void at the centre of this strange pairing. Like all narcissists they would feed their egos with countless acts of self-promotion, including printing their own fanzine, which was handed out free of charge in all the stations of London. It showed them trying on clothes, having their hair dressed, shopping and drinking champagne. They appointed two official photographers to immortalise their likenesses, with the aim of making them national, even international, celebrities. Page after page of sublimely retouched photos bordering on caricature, a cross between mythological deity and nouveau-riche snob.

Every part of the chic Belgravia house they had recently rented paid tribute to them. Their photographs adorned each room, and were even projected on to the outside walls of the building. The crowning point of the show was the giant hologram that appeared in the drawing room every evening from eight o'clock, at a time when passers-by could best appreciate the extraordinary spectacle. The performance changed on a daily basis to encourage the audience to come back for the next episode in this now legendary fairy story.

Behind this façade of artificial kitsch Puttock would drown himself in drink and as a result would usually be fast asleep before the curtain fell.

It was after one such drunken evening that Puttock awoke on a Monday morning, his breath like a sewer, his body soaked in sweat. The telephone had been ringing for some while; that must be the horrendous noise that had roused him, he thought. Naked as he was, he shuddered at the notion of getting out of bed. His partner was sleeping beside him, and the possibility that she might see him bathed in the light of day filled him with dread.

Finding a pair of underpants on the floor, he managed to drag them on under the sheet before emerging to make his way towards the ringing phone.

It was one of the Glimowitz brothers, who was clearly not happy.

'They've been waiting an hour, they're starting to pack up, you've got to come at once!'

Without waiting for a reply, Glimowitz hung up. Puttock had no time to trot out the usual excuses – his fragile mental state or other useful lies. Despite the titanic fatigue resulting from his hangover and the extreme exasperation he felt, Puttock realised he had no choice but to obey.

A RECEPTION ROOM IN A private mansion. Opulent furniture, heavy curtains either side of a vintage window-frame, and the restless sea in the background. A man sits in a large armchair, legs crossed, reading a book. He has a neatly trimmed beard and sports a monocle in his left eye. He puts the book down on a side table and moves towards the window, through which we see a breathtaking landscape. The man gazes silently into the distance, lights a pipe and exhales a large cloud of smoke.

'How did I get here?' He shuffles back across the room.

'I've achieved what I've always wanted. I'm a thinker, a humanist, a writer. My intelligence has brought me far and my looks have inspired whole generations of gentlemen in London.'

A waiter dressed in white enters.

'At last! My martini. Thank you, Winston.'

He sips from the glass and takes a draw of his pipe.

'Today I'd like to tell you about that culinary hero, that star among mushrooms, the diamond in the rough of the new wave of world gastronomy – no, not the truffle: the shining constellation, the unique and incomparable diva: the morel.' He gives a sneaky laugh.

The waiter reappears. He is carrying a tray with a bell-shaped lid. The man with the pipe lifts the lid to reveal a large fungus.

'In a single one of these lies the secret of absolute beauty – a powerful source of anti-oxidants that is the key to infinite youth. I myself am a living example of this wonder. The morel has not only given me a physique to envy, but also a scintillating wit and an intellect beyond compare.

'As the great Keats put it:

For 'tis the eternal law

That first in beauty should be first in might.'

'Cut! That's no good! One more take.' The voice rang out in the room.

'What do you mean, one more take? It was perfect, it felt right, what was wrong with it?' spluttered Norman Puttock, who in his agitation had spilt his martini. 'Take that away and bring me a real drink,' he roared. 'I said everything that's in the script, just added the Keats. I thought it would ease the tension a little.'

The technician stared at him wide-eyed, not daring to speak.

'Mr Puttock! Humility, we said, don't you remember? And I'm not convinced about the ending. We'll have to change it. It doesn't emphasise your innate modesty, if I may be so bold.'

'Drop the Keats? Never! Where's my official advisor? Finley! Find Finley for me!' howled the enraged Puttock.

'He's not there, sir,' came the reply.

It was true: there had been no sign of Finley for a while. He no longer came to the club, nor to the weekly meetings at the Suckling Pig.

Frowning, Puttock endeavoured to recall the last time he had seen him. But his memories were vague, and he had difficulty recollecting. Was it that day in Hyde Park when, in the middle of his speech, some of the crowd had bombarded him with rotten Scotch eggs in aioli sauce and cries of 'Puttock – What a twat!'? Or that time when Finley had dared to correct him during one of his endless lectures on the habits of insects?

He could not say. His brain was in a deep fog and the few isolated memories that came to mind left him none the wiser.

'We'll be starting again in one minute, sir.' The technician was in the process of concealing the microphone under Puttock's lapel.

'OK. Camera ... action!'

He took a deep breath and stretched to give an impression of quiet inner strength. In reality, his skull felt as if it were about to explode and he wanted just to get the whole thing over with as quickly as possible.

'See this wondrous little thing?' He held the mushroom in one hand, stroking his stomach with the other.

'Cut! That's all wrong! Look at the camera and stop scratching your belly! Take it again!'

Puttock, feeling the strain and covered in perspiration, continued.

'Did you know that every beneficial element in the universe can be found in this unique vegetable?' Clearly exhausted, he added under his breath: 'I need to eat. I'm starving!'

'Cut! What the hell's going on here? We'll take a break. Give him something to eat, for heaven's sake!'

There was a flurry of activity in the room. Technicians, make-up artists and dressers flitted around nervously seeing to their tasks. In this mass of humanity Puttock felt an unusual buzz, as if a voice buried under several layers of indistinct matter were trying to make its way to the dark surface of his consciousness. His extremities were swollen and he had an overwhelming feeling of nausea. All at once he thought he made out a strange shape at the back of the room. It was the silhouette of a man, tall and thin, in dark clothing and wearing a black fedora with a flat brim. Just the sight of this figure came as a violent shock. A sharp pain pierced his stomach and rose to his throat, which, parched, fought against asphyxiation. In a feverish trance, no longer able to distinguish shadows and shapes, he collapsed on to the velvety softness of the Persian rug that covered the floor.

WHO WAS THAT MAN. HE wondered, when he had recovered a little. The shape was familiar, but he could not quite place it. As with a case of déjà-vu he felt clarity and concern at the same time. The hat – he knew that hat from somewhere. That suppleness of movement, that slim form, those stringy arms with prominent veins. Was there a beard? He was unsure. Yes, perhaps the beard was hidden by the shadow cast by the hat. A short beard, a few days' growth only.

He was streaming with sweat. Rivulets ran from his skull down his face, which was red as a tomato.

He strode to and fro, with no real logic or direction. Perspiration had soaked his clothes, and he scratched himself like a plague dog.

'Where's the bathroom in this shithole?'

He stood in front of the mirror which covered the entire wall. Water gushed from the tap. He filled his hands and dashed the contents against his face, slapping himself hard.

Suddenly, his gaze fell upon the deformed figure in front of him. He stared at it with disgust and astonishment. Drenched in water, with his shirt untucked and slightly torn on one side, he seemed not to recognise what he was seeing. He was paralysed by fear and could not bear to face this filthy stranger.

'Stop looking at me like that! I don't know you. Leave me alone!'

'I've come to talk to you about Caspar Finley,' replied the stranger.

At the mention of Finley's name, Puttock began to tremble. He scratched his face, harder and harder, bringing blood to his cheeks.

'I'm asking you to leave, get lost, scram! Don't come near me, you vermin!' His cries echoed in the marble-covered room. The stranger met his eyes and did not move an inch. Puttock, in a fit of rage and panic, threw himself at the man. With all his strength he rained blows on him, his head, his chest; he ripped at his clothing and spat in his face.

THE TELEPHONE HAD BEEN RINGING for some time. His skull quivered at the slightest movement, and the sound coming from the living-room was unbearable. He looked around, as if to reassure himself that everything was in its rightful place. His partner was asleep at his side. The blackbirds in the garden chattered joyfully, and the air that entered the room had an odour of new-mown lawn. A deep sense of relief came over him. The phone kept ringing.

Having donned an old pair of underpants he found on the floor, he ventured to get up to find out what all the fuss was about.

'They've been waiting an hour, they're starting to pack up, you've got to come as quick as you can,' shouted Glimowitz, and hung up.

Puttock was confused. He gazed uncomprehendingly about him like a demented soul. Making a superhuman effort, he tried to recollect what had happened. Without success.

It was raining and the streets empty. Nervously, he looked for a cab. Where was everyone? Where were the cars, the buses, the delivery vans?

Soft music drifted out of an open window. A chaffinch here, a crow there, the whistle of a kettle and the clatter of a typewriter mingled with the refrain of the rain. He walked faster and faster. Of course the smaller streets would not be crowded, he thought. But when he reached the corner of Chester Square and Elizabeth Street, his confusion began to turn to panic. St Michael's Church clock struck the hour. It was ten o'clock in the morning.

Bewildered and disorientated he turned towards the north. Elizabeth Street, normally bustling with shopkeepers and passers-by, was deserted.

Suddenly he looked up. His breath stopped. A figure of a man wearing a hat, not fifty yards away, stared at him coldly. It was the same hat, the same sinister creature following him, shouted a voice in his head.

In a split second he found himself running for his life in the opposite direction, terrified. Like a raging bull, he panted loudly, his nostrils swollen and saliva spurting from his mouth.

As if by magic the shadowy figure with the hat

appeared ahead of him. Puttock no longer knew which way to turn. Whatever he did to avoid him, his foe was always there. He ran north, he ran south, but the man was always ahead of him. If he tried to dodge into a shop to get away, the stranger was already there, fixing him with a stare from inside the window. When he headed for the next street he could see him at the other end.

It was beyond his capacity to understand. All he wanted was for the nightmare to end. As he ran, he pinched himself and slapped his face hard.

'I'm dreaming, this isn't happening!' came his words, over and over again.

THE CORRIDORS OF THE ROYAL Brompton Hospital were silent. In the on-call room there was great excitement. The interns whispered to each other to avoid being heard by the nurses; the nurses spoke in half-tones so that certain details would not reach the ears of the orderlies. The recent events were the talk of all the staff. Since that morning the eyes of the whole country had been on their humble institution, and discretion was required of everyone.

The gossip was that security had been tightened and the PR department briefed on the importance of the situation. Journalists were posted at all the exits and helicopters patrolled the skies above.

At dusk the door to the main entrance opened and a spokesperson faced the assembled reporters. There was a burst of flashes accompanied by exclamations that rang out in an uproar.

'Ladies and gentlemen of the press, I have good news for you. Mr Puttock is now awake. His situation is stable. He was admitted this morning suffering from a nervous condition. That is all I can tell you for now.'

The crowd could not contain itself. Questions intermingled with confused facts. No one knew what had really happened.

'Maybe Puttock faked illness to get himself out of the morel business?' suggested someone.

'Is he doing this to win over the electorate?' asked another.

'What's the connection between Mr Puttock's health and the disappearance of his colleague, Caspar Finley?'

The doors closed once more and the journalists, frustrated, resigned themselves to making the most of the few crumbs that had been thrown to them.

Each of them tried in different ways to gain access to the building. Some of them feigned an attack of exhaustion that required treatment, others decided simply to faint. All that mattered was breaking through security and getting inside the hospital.

Puttock was in a bad way. Lying in bed, he looked around in disbelief, his face distorted by fear. Small, high-pitched moans came from his throat, like the cries of a young animal injured and abandoned by its mother.

'They tried to kill me, that horrible man, he must be a hitman, they want me dead, they want me to quit, they want me to lose my fortune, they want to take my morels away.' He was talking to himself. Curled up in a fetal position, he did not dare to stick his head out from under the blanket. He was tortured by horrific visions. The man with the hat would come to his bed, crawl under the sheets and whisper in his ear. He would tell him stories of devious betrayals that made Puttock tremble. Even though he covered his ears, the stranger's words echoed louder and louder in his head.

'Writer, historian, researcher,' shouted the voice.

'President of the Idiots!' The words rang out in a triple echo.

'The Morel Magnate!' said the voice, with a deafening cackle.

Puttock thrashed like a worm attacked by a beetle. The sheet covering him was soaked with body fluids, mucus and drool mixed with his sticky perspiration.

'What have you done, Puttock?' came the voice in his battered skull.

'It wasn't my fault, he wouldn't listen, I didn't do anything, he just fell.' A desperate sob escaped his chest and he clenched his sweaty hands. With such thoughts running through his head he collapsed into a delirious sleep.

Outside, the scandal had hit the headlines. The *Daily Telegraph* ran a story over five double pages detailing the hidden secrets of Norman Puttock and his accomplices. There was talk of fraud, the theft of national assets, forgery of documents and corruption. An investigative journalist, who had reportedly followed him for six months, was on the front page. Grave accusations and highly incriminating photos were published. Readers were treated to never-before-seen images of Puttock slashing the tyres of his competitors, or stealing a floral decoration from a shop window – with a caption underneath saying: 'Flowers for his own grave?'

Allegedly, he had misappropriated funds from his club, sold his logo to a snake venom company, and agreed contracts without paying a single penny.

A link to an embezzlement case in the Cayman Islands was established, thanks to photos published in the tabloid press, which showed him in an all-you-can-eat buffet in Georgetown stuffing himself with Mangkuang dumplings.

Even the morel business was revealed to be a scam. The fungus was in fact imported from China and sold at fourteen times the cost-price.

However, one charge in particular appeared even more damning: it was insinuated that there was a connection between Puttock and the mysterious disappearance of Finley. Anonymous witnesses claimed to have seen the two men arguing in a hookah bar in Barnet. It was reported that Puttock had been wearing a fez and smoking a pipe that night. It was the last sight of Finley. A camera at the corner of Friary Park and Queenswell Avenue had filmed him leaning against a lofty lime tree opposite St Katherine's church. After that, there was no further trace.

IT WAS A LONG AND distressing night. The nurses did not know which way to turn. The mental state of their notorious patient was seriously deteriorating. Diabolical laughter could be heard from his room. From time to time there was absolute silence, before the cries began again. They heard objects falling and a confusion of voices. In the early hours of the morning he was seen escaping through the fire exit, his clothes torn and his hair dishevelled.

A short time later a taxi stopped in Chapel Street in Belgravia and a repugnant character alighted at number 10a. His shirt was unbuttoned, and he was scratching his chest while uttering small moans. With flailing hands he inserted a key into the lock and looked around. A pustule had appeared in the corner of his left eye and boils filled with yellow pus covered his neck. When the door would not open he began to lose his patience.

'I know you're hiding inside! Show me your ugly

face!' he shouted, at the top of his voice.

In a rage, he threw himself against the door, then fell backwards heavily before crashing into the façade again.

Twenty yards away, curious passers-by were spellbound by this disturbing scene.

'It's the famous Puttock, the Morel Magnate,' came the whisper.

'And King of the Idiots, remember!' replied someone, and the group burst out laughing.

'What are you staring at? You want my photo or something?' snarled Puttock, as he resumed hammering on the door. 'Get out of my house or I'll call the police!'

'This is not your house, sir.' A police officer had stopped a few yards away and, looking concerned, was talking into his radio.

Norman Puttock did not seem to understand. His gaze switched between the policeman and the onlookers.

'I didn't do anything,' he shouted at the crowd. 'He provoked me. I'd just lit my pipe.' Heavy tears flowed from his swollen eyes. Every now and then a pustule would burst in his neck and the pus would spread over his skin, yellowish and slimy. A high-pitched howl accompanied each rupture, and several neighbours came to their windows, disturbed by the noise.

'You can't stay here, sir, it's private property. I must ask you to leave.' The policeman, visibly disgusted, hesitated to come nearer.

'Don't you know who I am? I'd be careful if I were you. I am the most respected resident of London. Take a good look at me, remember that face.' With his index finger pointed towards his own head, Puttock glared at the officer of the law.

Not knowing which way to turn, like a madman – wretched and deformed – Norman Puttock ran. The only place he could go to was his old slum dwelling, the hovel he thought he had left behind in a previous life. There, in the dark, sitting on his small, dilapidated couch, he would pick up the withered remnants of his failing memory. His sick brain struggled to piece together recent events.

Full glasses, empty glasses, spilt bottles, some thrown on the floor and shattered into shards. Then, shouts and threats from the staff, a heavyset bouncer with a long, black beard. Outside, the cold wind, and the sound of each step resonating in the silence of the night.

'Hey, Finley, where have you been hiding, you treacherous dog?' He felt the first drops of a downpour. 'Bloody rain, not now, not with these shoes, damn it!'

Then: 'Ah, there you are! What are you doing under the tree? It's not raining that hard. Afraid of getting your trashy clothes wet or something?'

He poured himself another glass of whisky and, with trembling hands, tried to fill his pipe.

A flashback came into his mind. It was Finley trying to walk straight along Manor Drive.

'Stop, Finley, you don't want me to get my shoes dirty, do you? Let's go for a drink. There's a knocking shop not far from here; you can get laid for next to nothing.'

Suddenly his heart stopped for an instant. He wanted to let out a scream, but he had no breath in his lungs. A tear dribbled from his infected eye. His pipe fell to the ground from his trembling hands.

He was reliving that wet night, the mud on his shoes, the sound of distant thunder in the air. An angry Finley let loose an avalanche of invective.

'Puttock, you're a clown!'

Puttock blocked his ears and thrashed his head around.

'A clown, a buffoon, a disloyal, servile lackey,' continued Finley.

'Stop talking, shut up!' implored Puttock, pressing his ears harder and harder.

'You want the truth about yourself, you want me to tell you, eh?'

'Please, shut up! I'm begging you!' He burst into hysterical sobs.

'Look at yourself in the mirror. Open your eyes and take a good look at your ugly mug.'

Finley held up a small pocket mirror and waved it rapidly in front of Puttock's face. The latter, stooped in spasms of pain, moaned despairingly as if at death's door. Stunned and half-blinded he raised his meerschaum pipe in his right hand. In a frenzy of rage, he began to punch Caspar Finley in the face, forcing him to the ground.

Battered and bruised, Finley showed no signs of life. His face was unrecognisable, his eyes like two cavernous holes, from which the blood flowed copiously.

For some time, London had been awakening to growing spates of vandalism. Every day, stunned passers-by would find a selection of well-executed murals featuring the illustrious Norman Puttock on the buildings of the capital.

Decorating the wall of a disused factory in Shoreditch was a lifesize painting of him – stark naked, with a morel in place of his head.

The next day, he was depicted on the side of a chemical toilet at a Stockwell Park Estate building site, urinating, a near-perfect arc jetting out in front of him. His head adorned sewer covers and holes in freshly repaired pavements. Sometimes it was just a part of his body – two legs, his profile, or his hand holding a pipe. People had fun adding their own personal touch by drawing the rest. In every neighbourhood, near and far, appeared monstrous figures, both funny and fearsome, attracting fascinated crowds. It wasn't hard to identify Puttock, even when the end result was more reminiscent of an ogre than a human being.

Every drawing had something recognisable about it, which delighted the audience. Sometimes it was so discreet that the viewer had to study it closely before finding the clue that proved it was Puttock and no one else. In no time at all a community of enthusiasts grew up, dedicated to exploring the city in search of new mural creations.

Norman Puttock locked himself in his party offices and refused to open the door for several days. Journalists and onlookers had gathered outside the building, some even equipped with chairs or mattresses to spend the night.

The excitement had also spread to the Narcissistic Idiots' Club. Its members were outraged, asking: 'Did he take us for fools or what?'

Speculation on the identity of the mysterious graffiti artist was the talk of the town. Where did the charming miscreant come from? How did he manage to carry out his work without being caught in the act?

In the Tube and on the bus, in cafés and checkout queues, animated discussions sprang up. It's a political rival, said some. No, said others. a secret agent of the royal family. Such large frescoes could not be done in a matter of minutes; and the use of unaccustomed colours implied a profound artistic knowledge.

On its front page, the *Daily Mail* ran the headline: 'Venice Purple breaks new records.' Inside, readers were informed that since this particular shade of paint had been used in the gigantic Shoreditch mural, demand for it had gone through the roof, with more than fifty thousand orders in just three days. Whether for their house, their garage or their front door, it was the colour everybody wanted.

Other newspapers had a more serious approach.

'The fraud of the decade.' 'How many gilded steaks to fill his stomach?' 'Puttock – the morel failure!' The covers vied with each other for scoops and exclusives, their depressing articles sinking to unexpected depths. One was particularly disturbing. The silhouette of a man had been captured in a number of photos. He was in the riotous crowd in Hyde Park, as well as in the audience at the Narcissistic Idiots' Club on election day. He could also be seen in the background as Puttock cut the ribbon at a shop opening in Mayfair. The same profile was identified in a blurred photo taken by a paparazzo at a sausage-tasting event in Swindon. In it, Puttock, surrounded by a cheerful crowd, his double chin drooping and his face twisted in a grimace, was eating a piece of salami. Behind him was the enigmatic stranger, a camera in his hands.

Detective Inspector Sharpe waited patiently at the door to the red-brick building located at 335 High Holborn. Like a horde of angry wasps the journalists were testing the strength of the barricade erected in front of the building.

'Calm down, please.' Sharpe gave a long press on the doorbell. When the door failed to open, he raised his eyes to the windows looking for help, anything that would get him out of this embarrassing situation. After a long interval, there was a beep and Sharpe disappeared into the dark cavern of the entrance hall.

On the third floor of the building, pandemonium reigned. Serious-looking men moved backwards and forwards. The ringing of telephones drowned out the chaotic conversations that filled the space, like noises lost in the middle of a snow-capped mountain.

High-pitched screams came from down the hall. Whenever one of these was heard, the din would stop and an eerie silence would ensue. Inspector Sharpe, noticeably ill at ease, walked the length of the hallway that ran from front to back of the building. The closer he got to the end of it, the louder the screams became. When he reached the door, he stopped and took a breath before knocking three times. Then, his palms sweating, he turned the knob.

'There you are at last! You're late, Sharpe!'

It was Puttock. Lying on a two-seater Louis Philippe sofa, wearing just a bath towel wrapped around his waist, he stared at the ceiling. His legs protruded over the armrest and their extreme whiteness, accentuated by the rays of the morning sun, produced a fantasmagorical effect. Baskets and dishes full of mushrooms, were scattered around the room.

'What on earth happened, Mr Puttock?'

The inspector did not know where to look. His attention was drawn to the myriad of bowls and serving vessels which, at first sight, were reminiscent of a 19th century still-life composition.

'Ah! I'll have another!' Puttock plunged his hands into one of the receptacles, then threw the mushroom into the air and tried to catch it in his mouth. He missed it; and gave vent to one of the unearthly cries that froze Sharpe's blood.

'Find me that unspeakable man! I told you he was real. I saw him several times. You believe me now, I hope!'

'The reason I've come to see you, sir, is to talk about the morels. There's a problem.'

A split second later, Norman Puttock was on his feet, his fury that of a madman. His half-naked body pulsated like a heart torn out by force. Enraged, he opened his mouth, revealing trailing strands of saliva.

'No one's going to take away my morels, no one!' And he stuffed mushrooms between his lips until his mouth could take no more, before spitting them out. Once the gobbet was ejected he began again, with even more enthusiasm.

Suddenly his expression changed, becoming more serious. Exasperated, he wiped the droplets of perspiration from his forehead. His breathing became faster and a nervous sniffle could be heard from his nostrils.

'By the way, where are you with your investigation?' came the weak voice.

Sharpe stared fixedly at one of the many paintings that hung on the walls.

'We don't have a lot to go on. We lost track of his

movements. And the CCTV cameras were knocked out by the storm.'

Puttock was noisily cleaning his pipe in an attempt to disguise his irregular breathing.

'But what is obvious, sir, is that something serious has happened to your colleague, Mr Finley,' Sharpe went on, with an unwavering gaze. 'He can't just disappear like that, drifting away like the smoke from your pipe.' A heavy tension had invaded the room, as if the air had turned to carbon dioxide. A searing cough rang out.

'Sorry, something went down the wrong way,' spat Puttock, his voice choking. The inspector continued, unperturbed.

'As I was saying: do you have any idea how many people disappear every year without trace? I can tell you that most of them either never come back, or if they do it's in a body-bag.' A harsh cackle ricocheted around the room like a bullet from a gun.

'Were you aware, Mr Puttock, that Mr Finley was planning to go away on holiday?'

Puttock, unable to conceal his surprise, started.

'And where would that be?'

'He had a booking on the Flying Scotsman, four nights, first class. He never turned up. And were you also aware that he wanted to get into whisky production? It seems that he'd been funding the Scotch Malt Whisky Society for four years. I'm surprised he never shared his interest with you.'

'I had no idea,' Puttock croaked in a low voice, his heart in his throat.

The inspector's gaze never left the painting, which created a tremendous feeling of unease in Puttock. What on earth is the vindictive creature looking at, he thought to himself.

'I imagine you're wondering what I'm looking at?' Sharpe's piercing eyes suddenly came to rest on Puttock, penetrating his whole being. He felt like a frog under a microscope, half dissected. His mounting distress tore at his innards.

'You see that little mark there? So tiny, almost invisible.' With trepidation Puttock approached the painting, screwing up his eyes.

'I can't see anything.'

'Of course you can. Look properly. Just there. The painter was trying to hide something. That patch of grey, it's covering something up. You get my meaning?'

Puttock scratched his forehead ingenuously. His face wore an expression of polite interest, but he could not prevent the occasional convulsive twitch.

'You, know, I never noticed that. I never suspected you were a connoisseur, Sharpe.' His face twisted in an attempt to smile.

'I wonder what could be concealed underneath,' went on the inspector, with an unsettling calm. 'A fevered brushstroke, a secret fantasy, maybe a message.'

'Ha, ha! I'd say it's more your imagination that's fevered, Sharpe!'

'Is that what you think, sir?' This time the inspector stared at him without even blinking, in that disconcerting way he had. 'I have to ask you, sir: where were you on the evening of the 28th?"

Norman Puttock's heart failed him. Or it felt like it. He heard himself screaming helplessly at the top of his voice.

'I'm going to file a complaint, you miserable bastard! How dare you ask me questions like that? You're going to pay for it!' Pausing only to catch his breath, he continued. 'I've told you several times, I was at home, stretched out on the bed!'

'Indeed, sir, that is what you said.'

A THICK FOG HAD INVADED the room. Puttock's perception alternated between dazzling flashes and hazy images. The sound of his own voice was drowned out by a terrifying scream issuing from the dark cavern of his subconscious. The multitude of portraits hung on the walls fixed him with a baleful glare. Inebriated by the dizzying light encircling his head, wracked with anguish, he felt as if he were in a sort of limbo. In his nostrils he sensed the odour of funeral incense combined with that of rotten flesh, together with a rather bitter sandalwood smell. It was like a sacred bonfire ruined by the hand of God.

His voice tried to force its way out, pleading for help with all its might. But his parched throat, like a deadly snake, was choking him: the cry of a mute, squeezed out into a deaf, distressed world.

'I didn't do anything wrong! Believe me, I'm innocent!'

Pronouncing these few words gave him fresh

strength. The adrenalin newly infused into his veins had reached his extremities and his heart resumed its normal rhythm. The simple utterance was like a powerful restoring drug. No one, but no one, should have the right to treat him so badly. Anyone who ventured on to such dangerous territory should be prepared for the worst.

'He's the guilty one, he's the one who should be arrested! I bet you he's the artist, the idiot! Have you seen his drawings, eh? Look at the shape of my nose: he's put a wart on it! And that gross stomach – it makes me look like a whale! Oh, why me, why? Didn't they understand that I'm special, I'm the only leader they need? The ungrateful wretches!'

Malicious laughter escaped from the misty cloud that surrounded him.

'It's me who's immortalised here. And there, and there!' He indicated the paintings on the walls. 'Those are the real pictures! Are you blind, for God's sake?'

At this, he began to run from one painting to the next, sometimes bowing before them, sometimes biting himself until he bled. He kissed his own flesh, licked himself as best he could, in an attempt to appease his need for sensuality.

A curious scent pervaded his estranged being,

like a poisonous bile. Layer by layer it penetrated his body, soaking into him until he believed himself omnipotent, like an unbreakable gemstone.

'No, not a sapphire. Not a ruby, either. An emerald…? No! I'm a diamond!' His delirious words came in a whisper.

Sharpe could not contain his concern.

'Forgive me, sir, but that's Captain Gilbert Heathcote. And over there is Lord Byron. They can't be you. I don't know how to explain it any better.'

Puttock was shaking like a leaf in a force 10 gale.

'But it *is* me! Norman Lewis Puttock, president of all the idiots in the world!' Plunging his hand into a leather bag he searched frantically before pulling out a card.

'Look! My card! And that's my club, printed on it!'

'The club is no longer yours, sir.' The soothing whisper that emerged from Sharpe's mouth could scarcely be heard.

And indeed, the idiots had held a meeting and voted to dismiss their president forthwith. The Glimowitz brothers were now in control of the party, since it was not thought advisable to leave

Puttock in charge given his current state. The posters in the bus stops and in the Tube had been removed, and his morel taken off the market. The fanzine recounting his idyllic life with Claire had fallen into disfavour with its readers. Enraged, they piled up copies in Trafalgar Square and lit bonfires. Claire herself – whom he considered his greatest publicity asset in flesh and blood – had left him for a dealer in Byzantine art from Manchester. She had assumed a new identity overnight and no trace of her could be found.

'What was that, Sharpe?'

'It appears you have been sacked, sir. It's on page one of all the newspapers. All over London they're burning posters with your face on them.'

Puttock looked perplexed. His fists were clenched, and his pipe dangled from the corner of his mouth. The lacklustre hair that drooped either side of his head resembled the worn-out mane of a horse exhausted by a lifetime of toil.

He felt weak and giddy. The floor seemed to be crumbling beneath his feet. The multitude of faces staring at him from the walls made his head spin. Suddenly, they blended into one, a single face surrounding him, full of reproach and hatred. It was that selfsame man, fixing him with his gaze. From every painting glared the same face, the same sad and dejected eyes that seemed to penetrate his chest before encircling his neck, leaving him gasping for air.

'I did nothing! I'm the victim here!'

He was choking, trying to call for help, but in vain.

Shortly afterwards he found himself in the streets of Holborn, Sharpe's words still ringing in his head. Like a spectral voice from beyond the grave they rose irresistibly to the surface, blending in a diphonic chant that pierced him like a sword wielded by a mighty demon.

'Where were you on the night of the 28th?' 'He had booked on the Flying Scotsman, four nights.' 'That small grey patch.' 'He was planning a holiday.' 'He never mentioned the whisky?' 'The club is no longer yours.' 'No longer yours.' 'No longer.' 'The night of the 28th?' 'Are you sure you were at home?'

After Warwick Conduit, he turned into Red Lion Street, then into Eagle Street before reaching Theobalds Road.

'Please, where can I go?' came the pitiful question.

Suddenly there came a dark laugh from the void.

'There's no place to hide, Puttock!' The laugh became a savage howl. Time stood still. Within his very entrails he felt a desperate need to run. He tried to move his legs, but they remained frozen, as did his arms and his throat, unable to utter a word.

Heavy tears welled up in his eyes. A spider's web of red threads covered his eyeballs. He could hear nothing, could see nothing. Minutes passed, seeming like hours.

Gradually, his senses began to return. His vision cleared and his limbs tingled back to life. Little by little, he became conscious of the noise from the street. The sounds of buses braking and ambulances wailing came in waves, before being replaced by silence once more. Someone was playing a barrel organ, a melody he seemed to know. bringing a mysterious pang to his hardened heart without his knowing why.

Lost in painful memories he walked against the traffic down Emerald Street. Car horns sounded irritably, but only made Puttock move faster. There, in the middle of the road, he could hear the terrible melody getting louder and louder, taking him back through the years to where he had grown up, lacking both friends and parental love. Having lived for so long in a working-class village on the outskirts of Birmingham was, he felt, a black mark in his biography.

Images of painful memories paraded before his eyes. He saw the marketplace, with its stalls of local produce and second-hand clothing. Saturday morning, everybody would be there, including the mayor, who every week organised a bingo game with small prizes on offer. And there was the milkman for whom he had never left as much as a penny on Boxing Day.

'Well, hello, Mr Puttock! What a fine day, eh?'

'Rotten bastard,' thought Puttock. 'As if he wasn't raking in enough, he has the nerve to expect a bonus!'

And there was old Wilson, sitting at a table outside the Cock and Bottle, one of the two pubs in the village. Now blind, he could scarcely make out the shapes that surrounded him.

'Wilson, old chum, what's that you're scratching at?'

'Mr Puttock, you've come at the right time, God bless you. Have a look and tell me if I've won anything. I can't quite see the figures.'

'Sorry, old chap. No luck! Next time, eh?'

He saw children racing around and dogs leaping after sticks thrown for them.

O'Ryan, the butcher, surrounded by an excited group, was holding a megaphone.

'Ladies and gentlemen, come along, come along! Try our new sausage: pork with caramelised onions. Hurry up, before they're all gone!'

An enthusiastic crowd had gathered around a table where two men were playing backgammon.

And Puttock took to his heels, his pockets stuffed with sausages.

'Mr Puttock, don't go! Look, I'll give you a taste of this mouth-watering sausage!'

At the corner of Old Church Street he went into the newsagent's.

'Excuse me. I've won fifteen pounds on this scratchcard.'

Puttock shuddered. The music stopped. Silence fell. The cars were no longer moving and the horns were mute. Then someone called out:

'Out of the way, idiot!'

Without realising it, he had spent hours wandering around the same streets, as if they were the paths in a blocked-up labyrinth. The last he remembered, he had been in Chancery Lane; how on earth did he come to be in Serle Street, he wondered. Lost and downcast, he raised his head – and stopped dead in amazement. The sight that met his wondering eyes was enough to take his breath away.

In front of him rose a huge multicoloured tent set on a green sward amid a scattering of stands and mysterious creations. Adjusting his spectacles, he concentrated on reading the banner above the entrance.

Across a spherical shape was written in navy blue 'Funnel and Crawley Circus presents the Extraordinary Freak Show'. And beneath it he made out, in bright red, the words 'The Human Morel'.

Mesmerised, he entered the tent and nervously took a seat in the nearest row.

A weird ethereal atmosphere filled the space. Very soon the lights were dimmed and triumphant music marked the beginning of the show.

In the middle of the arena stood a man in a spotlight. Dressed in a black three-piece suit, frock coat and top hat, he commanded respect and obedience. His words floated through the air.

'Ladies and gentlemen, tonight I bid you a warm welcome to our whimsical vaudeville, the most terrifying and mysterious place on earth, where nocturnal monsters meet and do their fiery dance until dawn, without fear of being subdued or chased away by what you call propriety. The cavalcade that will pass before your eyes this evening is the most wondrous thing you will ever see. Yes! Feel free to indulge your most indecent desires and discover your most extreme humiliation.'

He signalled vigorously and from the sides of the arena emerged a series of strange creatures, each one more bizarre than the other. Beings deformed by nature, wearing make-up and dressed for the occasion, paraded in a circle at a lively, comical pace, in a kind of macabre dance as grotesque as it was frightening.

Loud cheers rang out, as the room shook with a blistering rhythm.

'And now, ladies and gentlemen, get ready to welcome one of the greatest wonders of the world – the Human Morel and his disciples!'

Cheers erupted and the orchestra broke into a wild symphony. A fanfare sounded, a prelude to something important, and the spotlights played over the seated audience. After several movements back and forth, a circle of light came to rest on Norman Puttock's astonished face.

'So let's hear it,' the ringmaster went on. 'Give a big hand for his highness the Lord of the Morel or, should I say, the most famous human mushroom in the world! Let the festival begin!'

With a huge wave of enthusiasm the throng began to swirl in all directions. The ring, packed with performers, seethed like an ants' nest, while the orchestra picked up the pace, playing the same refrain over and over again, producing a magical harmony to accompany the perfect rhythm of the dancing and singing.

'Bring in the animals!' came the cry. A procession of wild beasts appeared, led by an albino tiger dancing on its hind legs.

It was followed by a two-headed snake, trying to juggle ping-pong balls as it crawled. Meanwhile monkeys in sequinned costumes capered about, clutching ropes and performing acrobatic leaps.

Puttock watched from his seat, unable to believe his eyes. His face was burning, his body seemed to be swelling up. Suddenly, he felt his legs move and his trousers unfasten themselves. The buttons of his waistcoat shot into the air; the sleeves of his jacket burst their stitches.

There was great agitation too in the audience seating. Bits of clothing were flying all over, accompanied by cries of surprise. Everywhere, men and women were being transformed into morel mushrooms. Their limbs were melting, and from the liquefied mass that was once their skin were sprouting strange excrescences.

Puttock struggled with all his might. He tried to make himself heard, but his body was now a spongy mass with circular or angular cells filling the cavity that was once his mouth. Summoning his strength he let out a wail:

'I thought I was the only one in the world!'

It was then that he opened his deformed eyes and beheld the people around him. He saw himself, everywhere and in every one of them. He saw himself in their faces; he smelt the odour of his own tobacco in their clothing. Inside his deranged mind, voices were raging.

'Who are you, Puttock?' 'How is your conscience, Puttock?' 'Are you afraid to die, Puttock?'

Solemn music signalled the end of the show. Heavy curtains fell from the ceiling and a subdued light came on. Howling with fear, Puttock hurled himself against the door by which he had entered.

He was terrified. Enraged, he took the route towards Waterloo Bridge, kicking dustbins and car doors as he passed. Next it was delivery carts and beggars' collecting bowls. A few yards further on he grabbed a cuddly toy from a baby, peacefully sitting in its pushchair. Overcome by wanton violence he tore apart the teddy bear like a wounded beast, barely conscious of its actions.

A depraved anger filled his eyes as he walked faster and faster. He hit out at a bunch of flowers carried by a passer-by, before grabbing an old man's stick and throwing it towards a double-decker bus. Then, turning a corner, he disappeared abruptly from the sight of the astounded pedestrians.

That was the last day on which the people of London laid eyes on Norman Puttock.

With the passage of time, the collective memory faded – initially into a blurred mirage, later to be replaced by the indistinct ghost of the existence of a being whom no one was willing to remember. ☙